I0529659

Guarding His Heart

Wiccan Haus Book 8

By
Carolyn Spear

This book is a work of fiction. Names, characters, places, and incidents are the products of the author's imagination or used fictitiously. Any resemblance to actual events, locales or persons, living or dead, is entirely coincidental.

Copyright © 2016 by Carolyn Spear
ISBN: 978-1-68361-111-0
Cover art by Fiona Jayde

All rights reserved. Except for use in any review, the reproduction or utilization of this work, in whole or in part, in any form by any electronic, mechanical or other means now known or hereafter invented, is forbidden without the written permission of the publisher.

Published by
Decadent Publishing Company, LLC

Look for us online at:
www.decadentpublishing.com

Welcome to the Wiccan Haus

Something wiccan this way comes to a mystical mysterious island where authors get to play and bring their love stories to life. At the Wiccan Haus you will meet Rekkus, Cyrus, Sage, Sarka, Cemil and Myron, all of whom return in most if not all the stories. Yes each one will eventually get their HEA as well.

We hope you enjoy the stories from all the authors and return time and again to keep up with the staff and meet new characters along the way. But fear not if this is your first or twenty-first story each book stands on its own.

~A Note from the Author~

Welcome to Wiccan Haus. I know you'll love this series as much as I do. It is a world of possibilities, an escape from our daily realities. An island with shifters, witches, and all manner of paranormal beings, there's mystery and magic around every bend, in each encounter.

I'm Carolyn Spear, mother of two sweet girls and wife of one fabulous husband. Reading, gardening and exploring are my passions. I don't really "write" but rather channel my characters' stories to share with others. A strange combination of small town girl, travel enthusiast and geek, I am thrilled to be a part of the shared world of the Wiccan Haus.

I love the characters in this story. Trevor Greene, is the ultimate in tall, dark, and sexy hero with a secret. His kind is hunted, making him distrustful of humans. Cassidy is a nurturer with a big heart and open mind. She has to convince him she accepts both sides of his soul.

I hope you'll enjoy this story as much I did in telling it. I'd love to hear your comments! You can contact me at carolynspear.romance@gmail.com .

A Note from the Author

Dedication

For my fabulous, supportive husband who lets me shut myself away from the world and still loves me. Thank you so very much.

Chapter One

Maybe it won't be so bad, Cassidy Sinclair admitted as the small ferry broke through the mysterious wall of fog. One minute she was shivering from the frigid unforgiving Maine gales that had battered her since leaving the coast, the next, a warm mist enveloped her. Now, she had to shrug out of the parka or risk melting into a puddle of sweat.

If only I could shed these memories like my coat. For the thousandth time in ten days, she tried unsuccessfully to block the haunting scenes from her mind. Her safe little world had splintered to pieces with the attack on her school. Some believed her sanity had shattered, too.

Warm breezes tugged tendrils from her ponytail. Impatiently, she pushed them from her face along with the tears that welled whenever she thought of the man who'd saved her. Tall and stern-faced, he'd quietly guarded her student, Allan Branson. She'd never understood why the boy would need a bodyguard and had never asked. He hadn't even volunteered his name. For whatever reason, it must have been necessary for his safety outside the school. Nothing would ever encroach upon her oasis where she nurtured the love of learning.

She'd been wrong.

Dead wrong.

She'd lost her innocent belief that day.

Determined to leave the sorrow behind with the frozen coast, she focused on the verdant island rising from the fog bank like a fairy-tale castle keep within a walled fortress. Inside the wall of mist, sunlight blazed brightly in a cloudless blue sky.

She glanced back at the thick mist now astern the ferry. This place seemed otherworldly, rising out of thin air.

Everything had been surreal since the attack at her school. Her hero had appeared out of thin air. He'd saved them, taking the bullet meant for her and Allan, her student. Try as she might, she couldn't tear free of the images....

Gunshots cracked. Terrified screams echoed in the halls. With each jarring report, the shots came closer. For a moment, she froze in fear, starting at each round. She prayed the shooting would stop.

It did.

The gut-wrenching silence proved far worse. She couldn't determine the gunman's location from the shots fired. Was he right outside their door, waiting for them?

Get the kids to safety.

She didn't consider her own safety as she silently directed the students out the window. Innocent little boys and girls cried. She shushed them, boosting them over the windowsill, whispering all the while to calm them. She prayed someone was outside to take care of them.

Gunfire spat closer now.

Panic rose, threatening to choke her.

Got to get all the kids out.

One by one, she dropped them to safety out the window. She struggled to control her breathing.

Her "shadow," Allan, clung to her leg like a koala. He refused to budge.

"I'll be right behind you, Allan," she whispered, attempting to pry his little arms off her. Desperate to get them both to out alive, she pinched his arm. He released her, rubbing the spot.

"Ow!"

His voice bounced off the walls. A part of her wanted to scream at the boy, but the teacher in her simply shushed him as she boosted him to the sill.

The unmistakable metal slide and chink of a round being chambered rooted her in place.

The gunman, all in black like some evil specter, rounded the corner and aimed at her. The ski mask hid all but his cold, dark eyes.

"Give me the boy."

Her breath caught in her lungs. She stiffened her back and stared at her attacker.

"No."

Instead of responding, he lunged forward and grabbed her wrist.

Oh God, please save us!

Allan's bodyguard appeared out of nowhere, tackling the assailant to the ground. A silver blade caught the sunlight as her hero slashed the assailant. Horrified but transfixed, she couldn't tear her gaze from the violent struggle. Time slowed while her heart raced.

"Cassie! Get Allan out of here!"

The command snapped her out of her fog and spurred her to action. Wiping her sweaty palms on her pants, she took Allan by the wrists and hoisted him out the window. She stretched as far as she could then let go.

"I'm okay" she heard as she turned and gasped.

The black semi-automatic jammed against the bodyguard's ribs—

The blast deafened her, freezing her in place. In an instant, in place of her hero, a huge, furry beast roared and brought the blade down, felling the evil man with one forceful stab to the heart. Both slid to the ground, mortally wounded. She blinked and the bodyguard was there, instead of the beast, crimson spurting from his thigh. From the volume pooling on the floor, he'd die in minutes.

She pushed off the wall she'd been glued to and hurried to him, pressing hard against the red stain on his jeans.

"Cassie. You should go."

She met his potent, sea-blue gaze, caught in how pale his face had turned, struggling to make the pieces of what she'd witnessed fit in her reality. They didn't make sense. One second, he wasn't there, the next he was. There was no way she wouldn't have seen him round the corner.

"No."

His eyes slid shut and his head rolled to the side.

Fear balled in her throat, choking her, as she checked the wound. It still gushed, so she pressed harder.

"Cassie, I'm sorry...." His voice, just a whisper, trailed off.

He was gone.

The boat rocked, knocking her against the rail and jarring her from her thoughts. Grateful for the much-needed distraction, she focused on the island ahead.

This weather was strange. March shouldn't be this warm, but she gratefully accepted the rays of the sun beaming like a beacon of hope to lead her out of the depths of despair. This last week seemed like scenes from a horror film.

A lunatic had attacked her school. When questioned by the police, she'd told them the man had appeared out of thin air. She'd told them the truth, and they'd held her for psychiatric observation. A doctor determined she suffered from post-traumatic stress disorder. Locked up for her own safety, held for observation, her only visitor had been Ian Branson, Allan's father.

Her time in the psych ward gave her time to deal with the deaths of some of her friends at work, but also innocent children who'd done nothing wrong. They'd been in the wrong place at the wrong time. Counselors had forced her to examine not only the events, scene by horrifying scene, but also grilled her on her claim she'd seen a man appear like a wraith.

Thank God she hadn't told the police or doctors she'd seen the rescuer morph into a hairy creature. They'd lock her up for good and throw away the key.

Unfortunately, she'd also had time to dwell on the passing of her father and how heartbroken she'd been. She'd always been a daddy's girl. When her dad passed, she'd discovered how little she had in common with her mother. They'd drifted apart, living separate lives under the same roof until she'd gone to college. Other than the yearly holiday calls, her mother was a stranger.

Mr. Branson was closer to a relative at this point than her mother. He'd brought her real food when he visited every day. He'd arranged for her release to a therapeutic retreat at Wiccan Haus.

She'd find a better way to express her appreciation than the muttered "thank you" she gave him when he told her. She'd find a way to lock away the heartbreaking images of a solitary man with a secret who had saved her and Allan. She'd find a way to move on, with or without the mystical help on the island.

Surviving her father's death as a teenager and her mother's emotional distance made her strong. She would survive this tragedy, too.

***

"What do you mean I've been reassigned?"

May the gods help him, he had certainly earned this break and rehabilitation at the island spa. He'd paid dearly, almost losing his life this time, which was saying a lot because he was hard to kill.

Trevor Greene's leg ached, even with the ointments Sage, the youngest of the four Rowan siblings who owned the island, prepared especially for him. Herbs were her specialty and she was a miracle worker, but his wounds required extensive, hands-on treatments by both Sage and Dana.

Not that he minded having sexy women put their

hands on his leg, massaging almost to his groin. Had Rekkus known he'd sported a hard-on when his mate, Dana, was working his weakened muscles, he wouldn't have much left to rehabilitate. Rekkus wouldn't care he was fantasizing those hands belonged to a sexy blonde teacher. The weretiger would eviscerate him without a second thought.

And since Rekkus, the island's head of security, now stood over him eyeing the pool longingly, he dragged his focus back to the matter at hand.

The huge man shrugged. "I don't know why, and I don't care. I brought you the message from the mainland when I picked up a special guest at the dock."

Trevor heaved himself up from the edge, favoring his right leg, and stood. Even Rekkus, at six foot five, had to look up at Trevor. He nodded toward the envelope in the man's hand, assuming it was the message.

"Are those my orders?"

Rekkus glanced down at the envelope with Sage's name scrawled on the front.

"No. Your message is verbal."

"When do I have to go back?"

A slight smirk curled the other man's lip. "You don't. Your new charge is right here on the island."

Special guest? Shit, is it one of the Syndicate's big wigs this time? Can't be. I can't even successfully protect a little boy. They wouldn't give me one of the chairmen to guard.

Trevor grew wary as Rekkus' smirk turned almost wickedly amused.

Oh, shit. It must be someone really pathetic for them to entrust their care to me. Or one of the teenage kids of the councilmen. Kill me now.

"Well, do you want to know who it is?" While they weren't exactly friends, they were both in the protection business and had developed a mutual respect, so if the man was almost laughing outright, it must be pretty damn mortifying.

Resigned, he hung his head and sighed. *I might as well find out.* "Okay, smartass. Who is it?"

"Cassidy Sinclair."

Everything in him froze: respiration, heartbeat, thoughts. Everything. Except that twitch in his swim trunks.

Rekkus' heavy hand on his shoulder shook him back to reality. "Remember her, I guess?"

How could I forget her? Her silky, honey-gold hair, those hazel eyes, that perfect body. He hadn't gone an hour without thinking of her. Before and after. After the attack. After his failure....

"I can't guard her. She thinks I'm dead."

Weak, but it was one reason he shouldn't be protecting her. Besides the staff on the island and the chairman's own security team, nobody knew he was alive and, for now, the chairman had decided to keep it that way.

Rekkus rocked back on his heels, his left hand jamming the envelope in the back pocket of his black jeans. "That's not my call. There is this one thing, Trevor." His mouth twisted as if he didn't know how to say what needed to be said. "The problem is that she's been in a mental ward."

Every muscle in Trevor's body tightened as he processed this new information. "You met her. What do you think? Does she need a psychiatrist?"

He waited while his companion drew out the

tension. "Well, she says she saw the man who dove in front of her and the boy materialize out of thin air. Of course, neither that man—*who died*—nor the dead assailant is around to corroborate her story. In fact, neither body was ever found." He shrugged with that careless air of his and stalked down the path toward the main house. "So what do *you* think?"

A full minute ticked by before Trevor's brain could engage in coherent thought. He dragged his fingers through his hair, yanking to release some of the tension in his suddenly tight muscles.

Fuck. Me.

Every epithet he knew flowed in a continuous stream through his mind and when he'd exhausted all of those, he created some new ones.

One fucking moment, I'm relaxed, recuperating from almost biting the big one. The next, I'm assigned as a fucking babysitter to the goddamn gorgeous teacher who almost got me killed. On top of that, she's fucked up because she saw me appear out of nowhere to dive in front of the bullet meant for her.

"Come now, Trevor," the singsong voice of the waifish co-owner of Wiccan Haus said, standing on tiptoe to kiss his jaw. "It can't be that bad."

Oh, Sage knew exactly how bad it was. If she hadn't been so good to him this last week, healing him, he'd have replied with more of those creative curses.

Instead, he bit back the nasty retort that danced like the devil at the tip of his tongue and curled his fingers painfully into his palms. The slight ache helped center him and he stared at her.

"You knew."

A sly smile played at her lips. Slim and pale, she appeared fragile. He knew better; she was as strong as any of her siblings. And sneaky. She'd known for days— maybe as long as he'd been here—that Cassidy was coming. Hell, she'd probably arranged it.

It wasn't bad enough he was a pawn at the mercy of the fates. When paranormals started messing with the natural order of things, his life would become an unholy mess.

***

"Thanks for escorting me to my room, Dana. I appreciate it, but I assure you, I won't try to do anything stupid."

Dana stared at Cassidy, her mouth gaping. She snapped it shut and paused outside room 313. "Why would you say such a thing, Cassidy?"

Everyone was on a first name basis here. Maybe it enhanced the casual atmosphere, made it seem more relaxing.

Dana seemed determined to wait for her explanation before unlocking the door as she stood there with her hand on her hip and a cocked eyebrow.

"In case you didn't know, which I'm sure you do since you're escorting me all the way to my room, I'm supposedly crazy."

Dana didn't reply or even seemed surprised.

"So, let me in my room and you can go on your way."

Again, Dana took a moment to respond. "Cassidy, you are not crazy, and you're not a prisoner." She slid the key in the lock and swept the door open.

Cassidy moved past her into the spacious room, complete with queen-sized bed, mini fridge, and loveseat. She placed her carry-on with the few belongings she'd brought from the hospital on the floor. The blues and greens of the linens soothed her as they were meant to. The bathroom was perfectly clean and modern and comforting, too. Fresh flowers graced the dresser, while candles and potpourri scented the air.

Wiccan Haus might be good for her. No. Wiccan Haus *would* be good for her.

Dana explained the rules set forth by the resort. All guests must take dinner in the downstairs dining room. No wandering the grounds alone at night. Daily scheduled activities prescribed by the staff were strongly recommended.

Cassidy huffed out a breath and raised her brows. These rules weren't all that different from the hospital psych ward.

"What?"

Cassidy eyed her. "What did you say you do here?"

Dana's smile was too genuine to be forced. "I teach some yoga classes, I assist Sage with treatments and the greenhouse, and I manage my mate, Rekkus." She lovingly rubbed her swollen belly when she said his name and had the whole glassy eyed, I'm-so-in-love vibe going on.

"Did you say Rekkus? That huge enforcer guy who met me at the dock? You're his wife?"

The other woman's laughter filled the room. "That's what I thought of him when I first met him. I was a little intimidated. But he's really a pussycat when you get to know him." She leaned forward and whispered, "Don't tell him I said that about him. He hates that." Her belly jerked just at that moment, and she splayed a hand over it. "Shh, little ones. Calm down." She fixed Cassidy with a serious look. "You are our guest here. You are *not* a prisoner, and no one here thinks you are crazy. And Rekkus was escorting you more as a protective gesture on behalf of the chairman."

"Chairman?" *What chairman?*

"Mr. Branson."

Oh! Allan's father must have requested someone accompany her on the island. It made sense. This was Mr. Branson's way of expressing his gratitude for saving his son. He'd told her many times on the days he'd visited her in the hospital.

Dana opened a few dresser drawers, displaying neatly folded clothing. "He also arranged for these to be delivered on the ferry."

Tears swam in her eyes but she managed to keep them from falling. No one had cared for her enough to provide for her in a long time. She cleared her throat to help cover her reaction.

"Thank you, Dana."

Her simple statement was insufficient for how rude she'd been, but it would have to do. She couldn't manage any more right now.

Dana squeezed her elbow, dropped the key on the table by the door, suggested she'd feel better after a nap, and left.

Cassidy opened the drawers and inspected the clothing. Mr. Branson had thought of everything; she hadn't brought much since she'd left directly from the hospital. Restless, she wandered the room and discovered a couple of dresses hanging in the closet before she pulled back the drapes blocking out the sun.

Why would they draw the curtains in the middle of the day? To reflect the heat? Keep the sun's rays from fading the furniture and carpet? You'd think they'd want to showcase that view of the magnificent gardens and the natural pool beyond.

And what was that cloying smell? Potpourri on steroids. Panic set in as the walls closed in around her, taking her to a place she did not want to go. The room suffocated her like the hospital room where she'd been imprisoned for a week. She had to get outside *now*!

***

"So, your appointment tomorrow—" Sage suddenly broke off mid-sentence.

Trevor knew something was up when the three siblings in the lobby reacted simultaneously, glancing toward the elevator. Cemil, the tall, male version of Sage with his blonde hair and calm disposition, strode purposefully toward the third elevator, the one that shouldn't be in use right now. Cyrus, the dark-haired brother of the family, raised his brow. All the humans should be napping due to the relaxing herbs purposely placed in their rooms.

Cassidy.

Sage turned Trevor so Cassidy wouldn't see him. Out of the corner of his eye, he caught Cemil gliding up to her and tucking her arm in his, like they were lovers.

A jolt of jealously speared through his body.

Sage whispered, "Be calm, my friend. Cemil is

only taking her to the garden where Dana will shortly join her." With a quirk of her mouth, she added, "She's still yours."

He couldn't contain the growl that escaped him. "She's my new charge. That is all."

"Sure she is, Trevor."

With a quick pat to his cheek that left him grumbling under his breath, Sage breezed away in her gauzy skirt. He wished she wasn't right. Why couldn't he want Sage instead of Cassidy? He couldn't forget the sexy blonde who'd occupied his dreams as well as his waking thoughts since the shooting.

Her hazel eyes had shimmered green, like holly leaves in a forest clearing. Their gazes had remained locked as she'd crawled to his side to tend his wound. He'd have died happily then, connected to her, her tears splashing on his face. Instead, he'd been rushed away from her by the backup team. That memory of her had haunted him: Cassie crying for him, kneeling next to his pool of blood.

Now he knew she'd been punished by her kind for telling the truth. Worse, his kind, paranormals, had put her in that position and she'd been alone to deal with both the confinement and the grief.

Guilt, hot and bitter, flowed through him, clogging his throat. Damn it, emotion had caused him to miss the signals of an imminent attack and had put her and his charge in danger; he would not allow those feelings to hinder his assignment again. Especially with Cassidy.

As her assigned protector, he had to keep it professional. Starting now.

Chapter Two

Keeping Cassidy in his sights, Trevor proceeded to the gardens, stopping and consciously blending in like a chameleon when he heard voices. He'd tried to explain it once to Rekkus; he projected a field around himself that cloaked his appearance and that closely but imperfectly reflected his surroundings. If anyone looked right at him cloaked, it would resemble heat shimmering off asphalt on a summer day.

Leaning against a tree, he relaxed into his Watcher mode.

Cassidy. Her name tumbled in his brain while his heart skipped a beat. What would it be like....

He firmly pushed that possibility out; now she was his to protect, and he had to maintain a safe distance. For her sake.

He scanned the rose bushes in full crimson bloom behind the arbor where the two women sat. A bright blue jay caught his attention as it flicked from branch to branch in its search for tasty bugs. Salty breezes carried the roses' sweet and cinnamon spicy scent and caused limbs around them to sway. The leaves rustled on their branches above.

Letting their voices wash over him like gentle waves, he didn't listen for content so much as sudden change in tone, indicating alarm or fear. He protected, not eavesdropped, and he was good at his job. At least, he used to be.

She's so lovely. Always talks with her hands. He smiled before realizing his unintentional inattentiveness to their surroundings. *Gotta stay on guard. Can't let my mind stray to how gorgeous her tanned legs look in those plaid shorts or how those ripe breasts rise and fall with each breath.*

He forced his gaze to Dana. *The gods granted her some dangerous curves. Damn easy to understand how she attracts Rekkus. Of course, when your soul mate shows up, it's hard to turn your back on her.* Her hand rested on her swollen belly that had rubbed against him while she'd massaged his leg muscles with Sage. He'd experienced the powerful kick of one of the cubs and secretly envied Rekkus. Somehow he'd been granted a perfect mate who accepted all that he was, embraced it and now they were expanding their family.

His eyes drifted back to Cassidy. In that instant before his almost certain death, with her refusing to leave his side, he'd been content he'd found his mate. For that moment, he didn't care she was human. He would die happy. Then, he'd been dragged from death's door to face the excruciating truth: women and children had died because his lapse of judgment, his inability to correctly assess a threat before innocents were killed. His leg was healing. The gnawing guilt for failing ate away at his soul. That wound would never heal.

He needed to lock down his emotions so they'd never impede his job again.

Feminine laughter caught his attention and drew his focus back to the arbor.

"So, is there a man in your life?" Dana stretched her legs out before her.

Bet her back hurts from being unbalanced with her huge belly. He knew he was holding his breath on Cassidy's answer and hated himself for it.

Cassidy frowned, her brow furrowing, and sighed. "No. I wanted there to be, but that's impossible now."

Another reason not to let his libido drive: he had to stay on top of his game. Yet, he couldn't wait for her to explain more about—

Boom!

The ground shook violently. Like an earthquake whose epicenter sat directly beneath the island. The initial sound wave vibrated through him. A second sustained roar built; it sounded like standing behind a jet engine inside a hangar.

Cassidy's eyes opened wide then slammed shut as she fell to the ground on her knees, her hands clasped over her head.

"Get down, Dana!" she yelled.

Dana leaned over her new friend, rubbing calming circles on the woman's back.

Going to her seemed the most natural response in the world. He wanted to sweep her up in his arms, comfort her, keep her close. The voice in his head told him to stay his ground, keep watch, let Dana do the comforting. She was better at it. His job was to keep his distance, physically and emotionally.

"What *is* that?" Cassidy shouted from the ground, holding her ears, now sitting back on her heels.

Perhaps the fact that Dana wasn't afraid gave Cassidy the strength to face the unknown. Pride swelled his heart at her courage, but he didn't have the right to be proud of her. She wasn't his.

Dana smiled, though it wasn't completely sincere. He'd learned over the past week a little about the human woman. She was a terrible liar. She blushed bright red and stammered. He wondered if she would slip with a comment about the portal the paras used to transport to the island.

Her brittle smile pasted in place, Dana quickly said, "Oh, we're doing some construction. A little blasting, a little jackhammering. They'll be done in a little while."

Only the "little while" turned to almost twenty minutes, during which Dana tried to keep Cassidy distracted by asking her inane questions like, "Are Meredith and Derek still together on *Grey's*?" and "Has Letterman retired yet?"

Eventually, Cassidy stood. "I'm going back to my room. I can't stand this noise anymore."

Trevor didn't like the noise either, but he couldn't allow her to go back to the Haus until all the paras were checked in and shown to their rooms. Maintaining the separation of the two until the rules and a sense of balance were established were vital to keeping the existence of paranormals a secret from the humans and the humans safe from the paras. Especially the vampires.

By the gods, he hoped a whole coven of vamps

didn't visit this week. Keeping his eyes on her and his hands off was hard enough, but those sneaky, rule-breaking bloodsuckers spelled trouble. Often they worked in pairs to separate the humans they thought appeared the most delectable. Hard to maintain a physical and emotional distance if he had to stick to her side.

Hard. That word kept popping up, and the more he considered why he had to keep his hands off her, the harder he became.

Damn it and damn her.

The attack might never have taken place if Allan's teacher were anyone but Cassidy. His desire for her made him weak. He would've sensed something—anything—that would have tipped him off. Instead, all his senses had been drawn to her and he'd failed to anticipate the assault.

Now he was so wrapped up in assigning blame she was almost on top of him before he realized it. Down the trail, Dana struggled to catch Cassidy but was in no shape to stop her.

With no time to create a diversion, he stepped out of the forest in front of her and decloaked.

That did it.

She stopped in her tracks, her mouth working like a fish's on the end of a line, opening and closing with no words coming out. Her breath rasped out; she was hyperventilating.

She fainted straight into his arms. He easily caught her and tucked her head against his shoulder. Her scent surrounded him, filling his senses with orange and coconut. Her warm, soft body molded perfectly against his. A sense of peace flooded his body, like submerging in a hot spring back home. No woman had ever infused him with the same serenity the forest gave him.

If only she were paranormal.

Cassidy, I wish things could be different.

He waited for Dana to reach him, and together they made their way to the Haus, each carrying their precious cargo.

Myron, the Romany gypsy who worked the front desk, looked up from her ever-present cards. Today, her nametag read Pete, and every time Trevor had seen her, she'd worn a different one.

"What's with this place lately? Human women must be weak—no insult to you, Dana. Always some willing para man carrying one of them around."

Suddenly, all the shaking ceased. The portal had closed.

Sage hurried over from the front door.

"What happened?"

What happened? He inhaled a calming breath and counted to ten, aware that Cemil and Cyrus had joined Sage and were awaiting his answer. Well, not Cemil. He was just being polite. As a telepath, he'd already read Trevor's thoughts.

"She was determined to come back here, and I had to stop her."

Cemil grinned. "The best you could come up with was decloaking her dead savior right in front of her?"

"Yeah," he snarled, "it was." Cassidy stirred in his arms, and he tightened his hold, keeping her close. He savored the innocent intimacy and hated himself for enjoying it.

Dana stood between the two elevators. "Your room or hers?"

"Hers."

He nodded toward Sage as he waited for the third elevator, the one reserved for the humans. Somehow, these siblings had charmed the elevators so that only humans could use the one designated to go to the third floor, and only paranormals could use the second-floor elevator. The first elevator was reserved for the siblings alone. No one knew where that one went.

"I could use a key to her room."

"How will you get there?" Sage asked, though he was sure she knew the answer. As always, he would just wait patiently, cloaked, for his opportunity.

"Don't worry about me. Just get me the key. She's not going to be an easy one to keep an eye on." The elevator pinged, and Dana escorted him to the third floor.

In the privacy of the elevator, he pressed his lips to her hair. She wouldn't know, but he would remember the silky strands caressing his cheek during the long, lonely nights.

He needed to concoct a believable explanation for materializing out of thin air that would not threaten her sanity. Or his secret.

Chapter Three

"**L**et me know if I can do anything."
The door shut with a click.
Was that Dana's voice? Who was she speaking to? Where am I?

Her fingers gripped a throw, and the mattress cushioned her as she rolled to her side. Sunlight filtered into the room, and dust motes floated in the rays like dandelion seeds on the wind. Her gaze fell on her bag on the floor.

My room. Wiccan Haus. My life just gets better and better.

Silence in the room was disturbed by birdsong outside the window and the slow, rhythmic breathing of someone in the room.

Fear seized her for a moment, clogging her breath in her throat.

Breathe! Dana would not leave me in danger. Probably a nurse.

She fought to order her memories. She'd gone down to get some air and found Dana. They'd walked to the arbor. The loud boom and ensuing noise had frightened her then annoyed her. She'd decided to return to her room. Allan's dead bodyguard had appeared out of nowhere.

Like before.

She must have fainted. She couldn't remember anything between that shocking moment where he stood before her on the path—decidedly not dead—and now.

Was he sitting vigil? The man who saved me?

Only one way to find out.

Slowly, half afraid and half hoping, she rolled to her other side. Butterflies flitted in her stomach, trying to escape out her throat. Her heart pounded against her ribcage when her gaze settled on the huge man standing with his back to her, looking out the window.

Even in shadow, this man had to be her hero. Same erect posture, same immense height. His tanned, lightly furred forearms had the same long, lean muscles she'd admired for months. His perfect ass was identical to the man's backside she'd secretly drooled over alone in the privacy of her apartment. Wavy hair the color of pine bark curled against his neck, just like Allan's bodyguard.

But he died.

She took a few seconds to calm her rattled nerves and concentrated on controlling her breathing. In, slowly, hold, release. Repeat. After a couple of breaths, her mind cleared but still raced.

Maybe my imagination is playing a trick on me. Maybe I dreamed of him and never left my room.

She had to find out. After all, mental health professionals had proclaimed her "unstable." She hated to prove them right.

Scooting across the queen-sized bed, she moved as quietly as possible, expecting him to vanish before her eyes the same way he'd appeared twice before. Surely he heard the pounding of her heart; it sounded like a bass drum in her head. What if he morphed into the creature she'd seen for a split second on that awful day?

Odd that she was more afraid her imagination was playing tricks on her than she was of the beast.

He remained stock still as she placed her feet on the floor and slowly stood.

Three steps until she could reach out and touch him. Make him real.

Come on, damn it! I can do this. I have to do this or I'll always wonder if I'm crazy.

A few deep breaths—surely he could hear the rasp of her breath. She gathered all her courage.

One, two, three steps then reach—

Oh God, he's flesh and blood. He's real. Hot tears burned her eyes before streaming down her face. Relief flooded her body, mixed with confusion.

What is he doing here? I saw him die.

Questions whirled in her brain like a tornado, wild and uncontrolled. Nothing made sense. She fought a sob rising in her throat and tightened her grip on his arm. He was real and alive, and she clung to that shred of reality.

His muscles tightened under her touch. Springy dark hair over warm, tanned skin disguised sculpted granite-hard muscles. His large, calloused hand covered hers as he turned to face her. In the late afternoon light, his face softened as he looked at her—or was that her imagination?

His blue eyes locked on to hers.

The same stormy blue eyes she remembered from the man she couldn't forget. The man who had given his life for her and Allan was standing right here in front of her.

"Hello, Cassidy. We've never been formally introduced. I'm Trevor Greene."

His voice rumbled low through her, her stomach jumping at the sound. Another sign he was real and she wasn't imagining him, thank God. Her erratic pulse skipped and sped; her breathing came in little gasps. Her fingers itched to dive into his short brown hair, stroke the light stubble on his cheeks.

I'm like a lovesick teenager. Calm down.

She looked up into his face. It felt like a long way, and she guessed he measured almost a foot taller than she. Those sea blue eyes seemed to gaze right into her soul. Would those thin, masculine lips part into a smile for her?

"You're alive!" she whispered, though it sounded loud to her ears. "I thought you were dead. Knew you were dead." She shook her head and clamped her lips together because she was babbling like a fool.

Embarrassed when her voice broke, she hid her face against his chest. She needed a moment to regain some semblance of composure.

Warmth from his skin blazed from her fingertips to her chest. His scent—fresh pine and delicious male—wound around her like an embrace. Her heart pounded so loudly, she could barely think, and her breath caught in her lungs. She forced a breath.

His loneliness called to her as it always had. Strong and solitary, he was a kindred spirit. He hid a secret that kept him separate, yet it only added to his appeal.

His body was warm solid muscle, and she slid her arms around his waist, holding on like her life depended on it. Her hero was one hot, intoxicating male. One moment more, she promised herself, since he had not responded. What would she do then?

Barely had the thought coalesced in her brain when his arms enveloped her in a tight hold. A soul-deep sigh expelled from his lungs. What was on his mind?

Trevor pulled back and with one finger tipped up her chin. "Cassie." Her name was dragged from deep inside him. Before she had time for another thought, he brushed her lips with his.

Thoughts ceased. Her mind shut down, and her body and heart took over. She opened to his gentle, exploring mouth, her fingers moving beneath his loose T-shirt and up the taut muscles of his back to dig in and hold on. She darted her tongue past his lips, drawing a groan so deep it sounded more like a growl.

His hand gripped her hair at the nape of her neck. He plunged his tongue deep, took absolute control, and plastered her to the length of his hard body.

Her mind short circuited. Colors exploded behind her closed eyelids. Her fingers clutched at the long, lean muscles of his back as the soft fabric bunched in her hands. Adrenaline coursed through her like lightning zapping her nerve endings. Every synapse fired with the sweep of his tongue, the nip of his teeth.

She matched his passion in her kiss, pouring everything into her response. Her breasts ached for his touch. She pressed harder to him, her nipples tightening, heat pooling between her thighs.

God, his body was harder than she'd fantasized on long nights alone, his skin warmer, his kiss more intense. He made her feel alive and sexy.

Yes. Yes. I want more.

She moved her hand south, but he pulled back and held her at arm's length.

Staring at him, her chest heaving with passion and confusion, she struggled to ask what was wrong. *What the hell am I doing? And, more importantly, why did he stop?* No intelligible words came to her.

He dragged a hand through his hair, his gaze still on her, his breath quick and harsh. So he was affected, too. He closed his eyes.

He backed away from her, his jaw hard, hands in fists.

Leaving her thoroughly confused.

He shook his head, his eyes closed, and his nostrils flared. "I can't do this, Cassie. I want to, but I can't." He started forward then stopped, his hand on the knob. "Shit." He slammed his fist on the door.

With his forehead against the wood, he muttered, "I need you to help me to get down to the lobby."

Okay. Strange, but okay. Strange was the new normal at this place. In her life.

"Trevor—" she began, but seeing the furrowed brow, the almost pain in his eyes, she simply nodded and followed him out into the hallway.

"Lock the door."

"Huh?"

"Go grab your key and lock it." He leaned heavily against the wall next to the elevator.

We have a searing hot kiss, and he wants to talk

about security? Whatever.

"It's in my pocket." Grinding her teeth against the frustration and stung by the humiliation of being rejected, she dug in her shorts and produced the key, then shoved it into the mechanism and turned. To prove it was secure, she jiggled the knob. With more force than necessary, she jammed the key back into her pocket then punched the down button for the elevator.

For a moment after he straightened to his full height, he looked down at her. His empty stare, the downturned corners of his mouth, and the heavy sigh all indicated a regret that almost made her forget her anger. Almost.

Bing!

Anger still burning in her chest, she moved into the elevator. He had to duck a little to enter to avoid taking off the top of his head.

A shame. He could use having some sense knocked into him.

Anger at being rejected was better than embarrassment for the need still throbbing between her legs. His scent still pulled her, her body still tingled from his touch, her lips still burned from his kiss.

Did I do something wrong? Is he taken? Oh, God, is he married?

The reasons for his rejection swirled in her brain. He was as into the kiss as she was; his erection as rock hard as the rest of him.

He waited for her to push the button for the lobby. The elevator began its descent, and she couldn't stand it one more minute. Her emotions spun wildly out of control. Perhaps it was dealing with the aftermath of being attacked in what she thought of as her sacred space. Getting locked up for what she saw could have added to her reaction.

She needed answers for why he'd pushed her away and for the magic appearing act. Maybe he knew the reason for the assault on the school.

She slammed the emergency stop button, stumbling slightly as the car jerked to a sudden stop. When Trevor reached out to steady her, she snatched her arm from his gentle grasp. Slight remorse niggled her at his pained expression, but she held tight to her anger. His rejection still stung.

She backed against the handrail and glared at him.

"You never explained how you just appear."

He returned her gaze, his Adam's apple bobbing. "It's one of the things I use to protect my charges."

Charges?

"What are you? Secret Service?"

"Not exactly, but I am assigned to protect certain individuals."

Too vague. And not exactly true. Certainly not what she saw.

"And Allan was your charge?" Her heart pounded now as she was pulled back to that day. She refused to get derailed. *The past is the past.*

"Yes."

From the clipped answers, he could have been FBI, but he wasn't.

"He's okay, thanks to you." He had to be wondering about Allan. He'd been the boy's bodyguard, always so attentive, so kind. No way he was only doing a job.

"Thank you for telling me." While his face was

expressionless, his voice cracked, betraying his affection. He did care about the boy.

Anger drained from her, replaced by resignation. What was left to say? He wasn't giving her answers, not the ones she needed. She pushed the button to resume operation and the elevator jerked back to life.

Once at the lobby, the doors opened to anxious faces, including Sage's.

She had one more thing to say.

"Thank you for saving my life. Good-bye." Tears streaked down her cheeks, and she didn't bother to wipe them away.

***

"Let her go, Trevor."

Sage had him by the arm, dragging him out of the elevator.

"Botched it again, did you?"

Damn, she was one observant bitch. He liked her, but did she have to rub salt in his open wound?

"Probably."

"Probably?" The smug grin on her face stirred the beast within. When he growled at her, she shrugged and smacked his arm. "Don't you growl at me, and don't even think about releasing your inner animal on me. Especially in full view of my guests. You'll give them a heart attack."

"I need to find Cassie." He headed toward the front doors, where he'd last seen her.

Cemil stepped in front of him and blocked his way. "Give her some time, Trevor."

As Trevor made to push past him, Cemil grabbed his arm and held on.

"So, my friend, she offered herself, and you refused? Women don't take rejection well. You need to give her tonight to calm down. Especially since you haven't told her she is your new assignment."

Cemil released him and stepped back. The siblings exchanged a look, nodded, and Sage glided away without another word.

"So, you found your mate, did you?"

Trevor shook his head even as his heart pounded the answer. *Yes. Damn psychics. Reading people's minds.*

"No. She's my charge. That's all."

Cemil patted Trevor's arm, a smile curving his mouth.

"Sure, my friend, fight it if you feel you must. You might take a look at Rekkus, though."

"I gotta go, Cemil. Don't go sharing your observations with your siblings."

I have to find her, damn it. She could be in danger.

Once he was far enough away from anyone, he cloaked and began hunting for her.

Almost immediately, her laugh chimed on the breeze. His stomach tightened because she wasn't with him; he feared she never would be with him. Keeping her at arm's length was his choice. She'd been willing—more than willing—to get involved, but there was so much she didn't know about him, and he was unwilling to allow anyone to hurt her, even him.

Chapter Four

The night seemed never ending.

Staying cloaked required focus and energy. Eventually, Trevor had to give up being invisible, but he still kept watch over Cassidy.

Protecting her would be a hell of a lot easier if she knew he was her guard and cooperated with his efforts. He seriously doubted she would cooperate with anything he wanted.

He needed to keep his distance. If he was right, and she was his intended mate, she would be drawn by the pheromone his kind exuded. This adaptation had evolved due to his kind's huge home range.

Cassidy ate dinner with the resident mermaid who served as the staff's marine security. He relaxed for a few minutes, decloaked, and managed a quick bite from Myron's—who this evening wore the name Samantha—plate before making sure Cassidy hadn't slipped from the dining room unnoticed.

Thankfully, she'd retired to her room early.

Sage had refused to provide him a key to Cassidy's room, so he'd set up in the hallway outside her door on an uncomfortable Queen Anne-style chair completely unsuited to his large frame. Every once in a while, Trevor rose to stretch his long legs and work the kinks out of his back. His wound ached and throbbed, and his eyes were tired. He closed them just for a minute....

***

"Oh, come on, you big idiot." Despite her irritation with Trevor, Cassidy felt sorry for the big man slumped down in the tiny lady's chair and had decided to wake him up and send him to his room.

Was he here to apologize? If not, then what?

He looks like a sweet little boy sleeping. Well, not so little. In sleep, his face—so normally controlled—relaxed, lines around his mouth softened, and affection surged in her. She longed to smooth the errant lock of hair from his brow. Just like little boys in her class who disappointed her, her heart ached to give him another chance. Her head reminded her he'd rejected her.

She shook his shoulder.

Trevor's bulging forearm swung from out of nowhere. He stopped a fraction before crushing her windpipe.

She sucked in a ragged breath as she fought his grasp. She dug her fingernails into his wrist, fighting his grip on her neck. Fear snaked through her as she struggled to gasp his name. He wouldn't hurt her if he realized who he had.

"Trevor."

His face, hard and determined, softened. His brows pulled together, and he blew out a deep breath.

As quickly as he'd attacked her, he pulled her into his arms, kissing her brow, her hair. "Baby, I'm so sorry. I'm sorry. You have to believe me. I'd never hurt you."

His words registered but just barely as her head spun. Yet again, she was on an emotional rollercoaster. One minute, she fought for air, the next she was in his arms. He intoxicated her with his warmth and scent surrounding her. Her head swam with the memory of his lips on hers. She needed to step back, separate herself before he could reject her again.

"Trevor," she began....

He swallowed her words as his mouth descended on hers. Heat sang through her, propelled by her pounding heart.

Oh, God, don't let him pull away again.

She ached for this physical contact, the release only he could provide. Something about him, his unique scent, intoxicated her, rendered her incapable of thinking of anything but him. Tension already tight in her belly coiled even tighter in anticipation.

His tongue glided over the seam of her lips. Tempting, but not demanding. On a sigh, she parted her lips, opening for him, inviting, her tongue meeting his. Had she ever wondered if his lips were too thin to kiss well? He definitely had technique and finesse in abundance. She had to break the kiss just to breathe.

Feeling reckless and loving it, she keyed the door and pulled him in the room.

Don't let him reconsider.

She pressed against his long, lean body, a ball of heat igniting low in her belly. Her lips sought his, were captured again, as he wove a sexual spell about her. Everything inside her melted and surged like molten lava.

His mouth moved to the sensitive spot under her ear. And the one under her jaw. Oh, and the hollow at the base of her neck. By the time she caught her breath, she lost it again.

She tilted her head back to look into his eyes. She needed to see him, know that he was seeing her. Glittering blue, his eyes stared into hers, his expression inscrutable.

Damn, not again.

As she started to pull away, to tell him to leave, he stroked his knuckles down her cheek.

Gentle and deliberate, he asked, "Are you sure you want this? That you want me? I'm not sure I'll be able to let you go after. I need you to be sure."

Oh hell. He hadn't turned away from her because he didn't want her. He wanted too much from her. Was she ready for that? Was she ready for a relationship with a man she didn't know, didn't understand? It didn't make any sense, but her heart said "yes." *Give him, us, a chance. You know he's a man of honor and courage.*

She smiled up at this gentle giant of a man. "Yes, Trevor, I am sure. I want you."

His mouth took hers again, this time with a desperation that bespoke a need transcending simple lust. His tongue swept her mouth, stoking her desire to a raging fire. His shirt couldn't come off quickly enough. The springy, coarse hair on his chest tangled around her fingers. Drawing a line down to his belt, she quickly unfastened it and snapped it from the loops. It dropped to the floor with a thud. When she went after his zipper, he grabbed her hands.

"Slow down, Cassie."

No one called her that, but she didn't mind—didn't give a damn at that moment—as he slid the thin straps of her short nightgown from her shoulders. The silky garment slipped down her body and pooled at her feet.

Trevor trailed a fingertip from one shoulder down to the rise over her breast, pausing to blow softly on her nipple. She sucked in a breath, forcing air into a suddenly tight chest. He hovered over the spot where her heart pounded against her breastbone. Could he could hear it? She could barely hear anything over the thudding of her blood through her veins.

He traveled past her navel and tugged at her panties. For a second, she regretted not wearing matching ones, but, from the intensity in his eyes, he didn't care. Her panties joined the nightgown on the floor, and he lifted her into his arms.

His lips plundered hers. Demanding, taking, enticing, promising fulfillment. With her legs wrapped around his waist, her desire was evident as her wet core pressed to his belly. She ground against him, needing the friction.

Embarrassed by her unabashed desire, she pulled back, unable to meet his eyes. She'd never been this wanton with anyone, not even her live-in boyfriend five years ago.

A growl sounded in his throat. Startled, she gazed into his impassioned blue eyes.

"Don't even think of apologizing, if that's what you were going to do," he said, his voice gravelly and deep. "It means you want me."

He tightened his hold on her, walked to the bed, and laid her down. His gaze caressed her naked body, heating her up without even touching her. He shucked his pants and stood still for her perusal.

She stared at his hard, tough body, her own muscles tightening in anticipation. She admired his broad chest, tapered waist, trim hips, traveling to sculpted thighs and calves. She couldn't wait to trace every muscle, every vein that stood out on his arms. This man's chiseled physique rivaled Michelangelo's David with one obvious difference—he was exceptionally endowed.

He kneeled on the floor next to the bed. What was he doing? Gently, he encircled her ankles and dragged her toward him, finally nestling his face between her legs.

A quiver ran through her with the first lap of his tongue on her tender flesh. If she thought she was hot before, she was burning up now. A flush raced up her chest and straight to the top of her head. He bent her legs at the knees and rested her feet on his shoulders. She lay open for his pleasure, but her pleasure ratcheted higher with each swipe of his tongue.

He circled her clit, flicked it, and her whole body jerked with an intense thrill. She panted with each lap of the flat of his tongue. She gasped each time he speared into her. He alternated the rhythm, keeping her on a razor's edge. She couldn't catch her breath. Didn't care to. She dug her fingers into the comforter beneath her but couldn't hold on. Her inner muscles tightened, coiled, bunched. Her heart raced. She bit her lip to keep from moaning.

"Let go, Cassie."

God, she wanted to, she wanted to do anything

he asked. Demanded. Hell, ordered. But she couldn't.

"I can't, Trevor. I just can't. Please, I want you inside me. Now."

The supplication and pure need in her voice convinced him she wanted to be with him. She didn't play games. She was good and sweet and probably more than a bit inhibited with her previous lovers.

He smiled as he rose to his feet. *That is something we can fix, but not now.*

After grabbing a packet from the nightstand, he crawled over the bed as she scooted back to accommodate his length.

He lay beside her, marveling at her perfect milky white breasts with the pretty pink peaks. He circled one with a finger then took it into his mouth.

He couldn't take much more of this. His cock throbbed painfully. His heart hammered in his chest. He trembled with every stroke of her fingers on his back, his arms. Electricity charged through him wherever they touched. He needed to be inside her as much as she wanted him there.

He sucked gently then flicked the bud with the tip of his tongue. He slid his hand down her body, over the curve of her hip, past the silky skin of her belly.

By the gods, she was so hot, so wet for him. No doubt, she'd be small, but as aroused as she was, their first time would be fine. Better than fine.

Fucking fantastic.

No turning back now. He stroked his fingers between her legs. Her body tensed around his finger. Blood surged his veins, pounded in his head.

Her explorations found his erection; she grasped

him firmly. She stroked from the base to the tip and smoothed the fluid over the tip. His cock reacted by swelling even more. He almost came in her hand.

He removed her hand from his shaft then ripped the foil packet and rolled the condom into place. After he settled between her legs, his eager member nudged her slick opening.

"Cassie, my sweet Cassie," he said between soft kisses. "I've wanted you ever since I first laid eyes on you. Now, you're mine."

Her smile turned to a breathy gasp as he eased into her. He paused, giving her time to adjust to his girth. Even then, her muscles pulsed around his engorged cock, driving his inner beast insane with the mindless need to take.

"Damn, Cassie, you're are amazing." With supreme control, he slid in another inch. With each exquisite advance into her tight channel, his ability to hold himself in check slipped a degree.

He distracted himself by feasting on her breasts, sucking them, grazing the tips with his teeth. Her hips rose. Her body fell to the mattress only to drive him inside her again. And again. Each time, a moan broke from her, her desire forcing her wildness to the surface, something he was sure she didn't even know she had inside.

With each moan, he lost ground in the battle with his inner beast. With a growl of discontent that he'd lost control, he rode her hard, deep, spurred by the pricks of pain incurred by her fingernails on his back. She met each of his thrusts, enshrining his cock in her velvet heat, until he hung on the edge of ecstasy. Close. By the gods, she would come first.

Her feminine whimpers became muffled as she

caught her bottom lip between her teeth to keep from crying out.

"Don't hold back," he ground out. He needed her to show him how much he turned her on. He leaned down and kissed her hard, swallowing her scream when he reached between their bodies to stroke her swollen nub.

He kept his rhythm, thrusting deep, unable to deny his body's need for release. She came hard. Her body jerked against him, her muscles gripping him like a fist, triggering his own unbelievably violent orgasm. He followed quickly, roaring in explosive ecstasy. His seed spurted forth in hot jets, draining him.

No woman, human or paranormal, had pushed his limits, had made him work harder to control his beast. Sex had always been a pleasant physical release, but never this grinding need to be with her again. And again. To never let her go. Could she be his intended mate? Could the Fates have chosen a human woman for him?

Careful not to crush her even though he desperately wanted to collapse, he lowered his body to hers, keeping some of his weight on his arms. He nuzzled his face in the crook of her neck, his heart turning over in his chest when she pulled him close and rubbed her legs over his ass and the backs of his thighs.

"You're really furry," she murmured, tracing circles with one finger in the hair on his chest.

You have no idea. He kissed her soft neck.

After a few moments, he withdrew from her to dispose of the condom. *I should tell her everything. And I will, when the time is right.*

He lay down with her, pulling her into his arms, and burrowed under the covers. He ignored the inner voice calling him a lying coward.

Chapter Five

Cassidy woke the following morning tangled up in the covers and Trevor. She shifted, trying to free her legs from the sheets without waking him.

Trevor.

Forty-eight hours ago, she'd thought he was dead. Even though she only knew him in passing, she was not only by very attracted by his masculine warrior appearance, but also his quiet, affectionate demeanor with Allan.

He'd make a great dad.

She glanced at the bedside table, where six—count 'em six—condoms had been stocked by the resort for their guests' pleasure. After all, sex was a great way to relieve tension. Wow, was it! She could barely move this morning because they'd used every one of them.

Had she made a huge mistake? Jumping into bed with a man she hardly knew. Sure, he'd saved her life but she didn't have to roll over six times to thank the man. Maybe he had someone at home. But he seemed like a loner. Just because he'd slept with her didn't make her his girlfriend.

She knew that but she didn't want anyone else.

Her heart skipped a beat as she remembered how attentive he had been yesterday when they came up for air at lunch. She loved the way he touched her—lightly stroking the back of her hand, tracing a finger on her arm or leg, brushing his knuckles gently over her cheek. Her skin tingled and she couldn't help sighing like a schoolgirl or smiling like a lunatic. She'd never been with a man who seemed so entranced with her.

He kissed the top of her head and pulled her close. He was doing it again. No one had ever made her feel so cherished, so loved.

Love. Is that what this is?

Weaving her fingers through the curly hair on his chest, she snuggled tighter.

Love? Yeah, she was going there. Not falling, perhaps, but definitely taking purposeful steps in that direction. She fought her heart's desire to rush in and dive off the cliff. Her body's signals were clear on the topic. Her head told her Trevor had so much more to offer beyond the sex.

Both of them ending up on an island she'd never heard of was more than a coincidence. More than anything, he held a secret. She didn't believe what he'd said about being a spy, and she was sure she'd seen him turn into a beast. He didn't trust her with his secret. One thing she learned from her mother's emotional distance was that she needed someone she could count on unconditionally.

She still had time to earn his trust. She prayed a few more days was enough.

***

Being with Trevor was as surreal as this island. She watched him over the rim of her coffee cup.

"I have to see Sage for a moment," Trevor said. Empty plates stacked in front of them proved they'd worked up a strong appetite from their lovemaking.

As he pushed back his chair to rise, she didn't meet his eyes. Of course, he'd want to see Sage. The woman was small and beautiful, vivacious and serene.

Her insecurities were only mildly assuaged by his kiss on the top of her head and the affectionate squeeze of her shoulder.

"Be right back, baby."

She tracked him as he approached the petite blonde woman in the lobby. He still hadn't admitted to his heritage, and she hadn't asked him. He had to open up and trust her on his own or they had no future together. Maybe they didn't anyway. Why did he need to see Sage? She hated that he would feel a closer connection with another woman, hated this jealousy that burned in her stomach and her throat.

She couldn't—no wouldn't— sit here while he spent time with another woman, so she shot from her chair and threw her napkin on the table. As she turned, she bumped into the geeky man she thought of as "the professor."

"Excuse me," she muttered.

He steadied her, taking her arm. His dark brown, almost black, eyes burned into her. Her skin crawled from the assessing look in his eyes and the insincere smile curving his lips. Creeped out by his expression and his forward nature—he grasped her arm for much longer than necessary—she again mumbled an apology, tore free from his hold, and hurried away.

Rounding the corner, she shook off the chill from her encounter with the weird geek, only to encounter a scene that fired her temper. A tall, strikingly beautiful woman with long black hair, dressed all in black stood alongside the pixie-like Sage who skimmed Trevor's cheek with her fingertips while he leaned down in intimate conversation.

Bile rose in her throat, but instead of running, she edged closer to hear.

"So, Trev," the brunette said, "easier to keep an eye on your new charge when she's in your bed?"

He drew back. Though she couldn't hear what he said, she did catch the unknown woman's reply.

"I'm just saying it definitely makes your job easier. Easier to know where your sheath is when your dagger's in it."

Laughter rang in Cassidy's ears as she stormed to the front desk. The card-flipping gypsy woman glanced up, but continued turning cards almost automatically. The woman's nametag was wrong: it said Rekkus. Was everyone here playing with her?

"Turn left, up the hill about a fifteen-minute walk."

What? She hadn't asked a question. Yet. "Wait a minute. Are you psychic?"

The gypsy smirked. "Me? No. But the cards tell me what I need to know."

"I wish they could tell me." This crazy island was turning out to be more of an asylum than the one she'd left on the mainland.

The woman's smile turned gentle and appeared

genuine. "The cards only tell me the possibilities. You, my friend, decide your fate. Your path."

Cassidy shook her head, the kind words touching deeply enough to break through the fury to expose the hurt beneath.

With tears now flowing, pissing her off even more, she muttered a thank you and made her way out the building.

Damn him. He was a bastard for taking advantage of her. As she stomped along the path, her anger dissipated, replaced with self-blame. She should have known better than to expect anything from such an attractive man. A player. Or maybe he needed more than what she was.

She shouldn't have assumed they were exclusive. Being together these last few days, sharing a traumatic experience, feeling whole and cherished when she was with him made her feel like they were meant to be together. Like fate. But that was crazy. And she was tired of being crazy.

And what the hell did Sage mean "his charge?" So, his job was to protect her now? Was getting her into bed just a part of the job or a fringe benefit? Well, she didn't need his protection.

Only a few more days to avoid him. She'd tell him to leave her alone. Go spend his time with Sage Rowan or whomever the hell else he desired. Stay the hell out of her life.

Disappointment outranked the hurt and pain by the time she arrived at the waterfall.

The flowing water and lulling sound soothed her. She wasn't completely relieved of all that pained her, but this place instilled solace in her.

Glancing around, half expecting to sense her

bodyguard nearby, she kicked off her shoes and sank her feet into the luxuriant moss. The rushing water drowned out her critical inner voice berating her for believing in yet another person who'd let her down. No, this was here. This was now.

She would get over him and push past the pain the same way she'd gotten over her father's death.

***

"Myron," Trevor began as he tried to hold the raucous laugh inside and failed, "you know Rekkus will not find that amusing." He jerked his chin toward her chest where the bogus nametag was pinned.

Her mouth and eyebrow twitched up in tandem as she replied, "It was the first one I grabbed. I'm not trying to piss him off."

Yeah, right. He wasn't fooled as the grin she attempted to suppress spread across her face.

"But back to why you are here?" Myron sat back and flipped over another of her seemingly ordinary cards.

"Blackjack," he said as he watched her turn over an ace of diamonds and a king of spades. "Hey, have you seen Cassidy—"

"Not blackjack, Trevor, but a mixed message." Her brow furrowed as she stared at the cards then back at him. "A package or a message will arrive, very important, but an influential man may get in the way."

"What the hell does that mean?" The mystical and mischievous desk clerk exasperated him. Concerned for Cassidy, he needed to know her whereabouts.

The woman leaned back in her chair, serene again as she shuffled the cards. "I just read the cards, Trevor. It's up to you to figure how the message applies to your current situation."

Her careless shrug infuriated him. He needed to know where his charge was. Now. After counting to ten, he tried again.

"Myron—or Rekkus—can you please tell me if you've seen Cassidy Sinclair?"

She took her time answering his simple question. "Yes. Yes, I have seen her."

"Today? Recently?" His blood pressure shot up as he struggled to calm down.

"Yes, just a few minutes ago."

Finally, he was getting somewhere.

With sarcasm dripping from his words like blood from a vamp's fangs, he asked, "Could you tell me in which direction she went?"

She pissed him off with another careless shrug. "Sure, she headed toward the waterfall."

He didn't bother to thank her for her help since he'd had to extract it from her so painfully. His giant stride ate up the distance between Myron and the exit.

"Oh, to say she was angry would be to put it mildly."

Great. Just fucking great.

So, she'd disappeared, she hadn't found him to tell him where she was going, and she was ticked. Nothing like an angry female to make your day.

Stalking out the door, he shouldered past Rekkus.

"Hey. Watch where you're going." His tone was low and deadly.

Even though his friend's face was neutral, Trevor wasn't a match to Rekkus's gift from the Fates: super strength, both in human and shifted forms. His best option was to calm down, apologize, and maybe Rekkus could help him find his woman. Damn it. Not his woman, his charge.

He should stop thinking of her as his. If he didn't keep his head in the game, he'd miss another signal things were amiss, and this time his charge would die. He couldn't let that happen—not to Cassie.

While he'd given his heart to her in the last day and a half, he hadn't given her his trust. He still hadn't told her his biggest secret. He'd had this internal argument a hundred times. He needed her and loved her, but he couldn't trust any human. Still, the thought of her with another man, bearing his children, twisted his insides and made his heart ache painfully in his chest.

After a deep inhalation to clear his head, he spoke. "Man, I'm sorry. I can't find Cassie and Myron said she's headed to the waterfall."

Rekkus dropped his hand from Trevor's arm and smiled. "Ah, so it's 'Cassie' now, is it? I'm sure she's fine, my friend."

Shit, he didn't need this right now. "It's not like that—"

"Oh, sure it is." The unfamiliar wide smile spread on the man's face, further irritating Trevor. "I'm the same way about Dana. I can handle anything with a cold, clear head. Add her to the equation and I'm ready to rip someone's throat out." He patted Trevor on the shoulder. "It gets better after you're mated."

Trevor stepped away, distancing himself from the concept he'd battled with many times since he'd first seen Cassidy Sinclair.

"Can't happen, Rekkus. Not for me."

For the second time in a few short minutes, amusement laced a staff member's voice. "The fates choose your mate. That's how it is for paranormals. The sooner you quit fighting it, the better off you'll be."

Chapter Six

Ten minutes of hiking brought him to the forested edge of the pool at the base of the waterfall. Here, he was in his element, surrounded by the rustling of the wind through the branches, the rushing water over the rocks, and the smells of the pine, oak, and cedar. The tension in his muscles faded as though the river washed it away. Here he could breathe and think clearly.

As he filled his lungs with air, he caught her scent. Citrus, soap, and woman. *My woman.* Cassie.

Shut up.

There she was, her skirt hiked up, showing a tantalizing view of her creamy thighs and those muscular calves. The sight of her made his knees weak and his breath quicken. His cock swelled against his fly from a flashback of how she'd tightly wrapped her legs around his hips.

She picked her way across stones in the shallow section of the pool just as he'd seen forest faeries do. His breath caught in his throat. What would she think if he told her of the comparison? His heart beat faster, and he yearned to tell her. He wouldn't, of course. Paras kept their world secret from the humans.

Especially the Watchers.

He hated what most humans called his kind. Bigfoot. Native Americans were the only humans who respected and revered his people, considering them "elder brothers." They were Watchers and always would be, never communing with humans who hunted them. Only the ability to simulate their surroundings and their super senses allowed his kind to exist in mystery alone.

Yet, his heart and body longed for this woman who embodied everything good: kindness, spirit, courage, love, passion. How could he properly protect her—as was his duty—with his emotions mucking up his ability to sense danger?

He blended into the woods, engaging his ability to camouflage barely a moment before she glanced in his direction. Had she heard him? Seen him? He'd been careful, choosing just the mossy spots to deaden the sound of his approach.

Had he lost his edge by falling for her? The realization jarred him.

He was in love with her.

Shit.

What a cluster fuck. How could he ask for another assignment? Telling her the truth was impossible without sharing all his secrets. She was human; she'd never accept him for all that he was.

Damn it. He'd known the first time he'd seen her dressed in her simple pants, clogs, and button-down shirt. How business casual made him hot, he didn't know, but he'd been instantly infatuated. Wait—too nice a word. Horny. Needy. Hot for her.

Even the way she moved turned him on. If she'd been wearing a nun's habit, he'd have wanted to take her against the wall.

Sick, that's what I am. Wanting to sink into his charge's first-grade teacher. Sweep all the papers and take her on top of her desk. Or the floor. Anywhere. Invisibly guarding Allan had been so fucking hard— all pun intended. While she'd interacted so sweetly and innocently with those little children, he'd wanted her with an intensity he couldn't explain or escape. Seven months of watching and desiring her while cloaked during the school day. He was supposed to be guarding Allan, but much of the time the boy stuck so close to her, he'd had no choice but to watch her, too.

Cassidy reached the other side and edged closer to the falls. Mist thrown up by the frothing white water at the base of the falls shrouded the weeping willows and ferns, turning them from green to gray.

Was she humming? Hard to tell with the roaring of the falls drowning out all other sounds.

Was she going under the water? Fully clothed?

When her back was turned, he edged closer, barely breathing.

She stepped on a narrow ledge behind the waterfall and followed it until she stood behind it. Her image shimmered through the sheet of water as her fingers traced shapes in it. Minutes passed and he grew anxious, fearing what she might do next. Then she stepped off the ledge.

His breath caught as Cassie disappeared beneath the surface. With dread in his heart, he fought the urge to jump in after her. After what felt like a lifetime, she popped to the surface and flipped her hair back from her face.

She'd scared the living shit out of him, and he hated feeling fear.

This situation was untenable. He'd always had the ability to distance himself from his protectee, yet he'd let that little damaged boy into his heart. Look what had happened with that. He'd almost gotten the boy killed. Now his charge was the human woman he needed with every fiber of his being but couldn't trust.

Still, he couldn't take his eyes off her. His charge was so damn sexy. *Just look at her, lips glistening, rounded breasts heaving under the bodice now plastered to her body.* What the hell had the chairman been thinking, assigning him to protect her?

His cock throbbed as she climbed from the pool, providing him with a fine view of her ample cleavage. Could he leave her alone and do his job after he'd taken her to bed? He'd have to. The occasional twinge of pain in his leg wouldn't allow him to forget his failure.

Cassidy wrung out her skirt and hair as she passed him. He froze as she paused near him; her head swiveled as though she heard or saw something. Had he moved? Alerted her to his presence?

Slowly, she moved on, walking along the path back to the Haus with that long-legged gait of hers.

Loved. Damn it, he had to stop using that word to describe anything that had to do with Cassie.

He probably should quit calling her by his pet name for her, too. Be more professional—

A gawky man approached Cassie. *What the fuck does he want?*

Why is she smiling at him that way? Fuck me, my emotions are all over the place.

He hung back while Cassidy politely disentangled herself from the uninvited hand covering her arm.

He's not hurting her and she's leaving, so calm the fuck down.

When she entered the lobby, he slid up much closer. He'd have to get in the elevator with her since he couldn't access it by himself. *Damn those ubercautious siblings. Couldn't they just do alternating weeks to keep the humans and paras apart?*

Holding his breath, he silently crept behind her into the lift. He flattened his back against the wall. She stayed near the doors and quickly exited as soon as they opened. He kept pace with her in camouflage mode.

How am I going to get in her room? There's no way she's going to leave her door open just in case an invisible man needs to get in.

To his great relief, she unlocked and threw open the door. He hurried through and took up a spot against the wall in the corner of the room when she dropped her key.

By all that was holy, he hoped she didn't undress in front of him. All the blood in his brain was already on its way south from being alone in the same room with her in those clinging wet clothes molded to her curves. He had to keep his wits about him, and he couldn't do that if his brain disengaged due to lack of blood flow.

While taking slow and shallow breaths, he tried to minimize the shimmer that occurred whenever he moved. It could be a dead giveaway to anyone who knew what to look for. Even so, he swore the blood pounding in his veins had to be audible.

Focusing on a spot on the opposite wall—after all he was here as her protector—he couldn't help but notice her unbuttoning her shirt. He held his breath when she shimmied out of her skirt and let it plop on the floor to form a wet pool at her bare feet. When she reached around to unfasten her soaked bra, he lost control and sucked in a breath. Hell, he barely managed to focus enough to maintain his cloaking.

The lacy bra hit the floor, followed immediately by her matching panties. His pulse raced, his heart thumped, and blood pounded in his head. To hell with strictly professional, he was outright staring.

Her breasts—so round, so firm, so full—bounced slightly as she glided toward the bed. *Maybe she's going to take a nap.*

Then his mouth dropped open, and his heart thudded against his ribs.

She lowered to the edge of the bed, facing him, her legs spread apart slightly. She loosened her hair from its pins, and it cascaded down to her shoulders. Her fingers traveled down her neck and stroked her nipples before lightly tweaking the perfect pink peaks.

Oh. My. God.

He closed his eyes, counting first to ten then all the way to one hundred to keep enough focus on remaining invisible. If she was angry before, she'd be furious he'd sneaked into her room without her permission.

When he'd calmed his nerves enough, he opened his eyes to discover she'd lain back on the bed, one hand stroking the tender skin of her inner thigh.

His inner beast clawed for release. She obviously wanted sexual release. He could give her that and more. Much more.

Duty. Honor. Protect her at all costs.

When her knees fell apart, her fingers lightly stroking her folds, his brain short circuited. He had no idea how she couldn't see him because he couldn't have any functioning brain cells left. Her hips rose as first one finger slid inside her core, then another while the other hand kneaded at her breast. A soft moan came from her open lips, and he bit back his own. He fought the urge to slide his hand down to his cock that pulsed impatiently against his fly.

Was she thinking about him? Or maybe that guy from earlier? Jealousy, hot and furious, flooded his veins. He shouldn't care who she thought about when she masturbated. But he did care, and he couldn't deny the longing that surged through him.

After a difficult moment of struggling to control himself, he was surprised when she stood to turn off the lamp. The lamp on the table right next to him.

Shit! Freeze and don't breathe.

He became a statue. As she clicked the switch, her breasts jiggled and her perfect ass—so muscular— flexed, nearly pushing him over the edge.

With the light suddenly extinguished, he no longer had the advantage. Closing his eyes to force his vision to adjust more quickly, he almost jumped at the warmth of her fingertips unfastening the buttons on his shirt. He sucked in air like a bellows.

"Trevor," she whispered between soft kisses as she uncovered his hair-covered chest, "just like you know my scent, I know yours."

He hissed as she took one of his nipples between her teeth and gently bit down, soothing afterward with her tongue.

"That show was for me?" he said, his voice gravely from restrained lust.

He should be irritated and exasperated that she beat him at this own game, that she played him. When she'd paused next to him at the waterfall, she'd discovered his presence. But, hell, her mouth felt so damn good on his skin, and his body reminded him she was made for him. He couldn't summon anything but lust.

"It was. How did you feel watching me?"

Her lips traveled to his navel, paused there to shock him with a lick, then followed the trail of hair to his rock-hard shaft. In the darkness, only the rasp of her tongue on him existed. It circled the head, licking with broad strokes until she took him into her mouth.

So soft, so damn hot. Holding back was torture. He strained against jolting forward. He was too big for her to take fully, so he remained as still as possible, letting her do what she pleased.

"Well?"

"Huh?"

Her soft chuckle vibrated on his cock, sending a shock of pleasure up his spine.

"Did you like watching me?" she repeated, tracing the vein on the underside of his penis.

"Yeah. Oh, yeah, Cassie. You know how much I want you."

"No." Her voice was right in front of him. "Show me."

The cloak vanished along with his control and

most of his sanity. Before his brain could reengage and scold him for not performing his duty, he peeled off the already unbuttoned shirt and removed the shorts and boxers. He grabbed her rounded ass and devoured her. She writhed beneath him.

What the hell was she doing? She should be mad at him, she should be screaming at him, not moaning as his mouth ravaged her breasts. She should, but she wasn't, and she'd think about that after.

He found her core and stroked and filled with first one then two fingers, providing the rhythm she needed. Yesterday, he'd proven to be a sensitive and giving lover. Today, he proved demanding and masterful. And, God help her, she loved every minute of his frenzied attack.

He flicked his tongue and she jerked in electric delight as his fingers plunged, bringing her to a fast and furious climax. With her brain total mush, her breathing ragged, she gasped when he drove into her.

Her scream jolted him enough to ask gruffly, "Are you okay?"

Okay? She'd never be okay again. Her need for him outweighed all common sense as she lifted her hips for fulfillment.

"Trevor, please...." Her tone must have satisfied him, for he rocked into her again, hard and deep.

Only his feral groans answered her feminine whimpers as he set a relentless pace. Her whimpers turned to deep moans.

Oh God, she couldn't take any more pleasure. Surely, she was coming apart. And then she did, her scream echoing against the walls, an overwhelming relaxation washing through her like lava. All her limbs went numb, heavy, every part of her except that bundle of nerves still excited as Trevor chased his own release.

He tensed, plunging deep into her three more times, roaring. She'd never heard him make such a wild sound, but she wasn't frightened. He collapsed on top of her, trapping her between his perspiration-coated body and the bedspread.

She closed her eyes, exhausted from their frantic coupling. She dragged each breath in then forced it out, her body still full of him. How could she fall in love with someone who was dishonest with her, who didn't trust her?

Tears streaked down her cheeks, and she didn't care. Couldn't care anymore. She would have to go home and forget him. Tell him to leave her alone and release him from the duty he hadn't even shared with her.

She'd gambled with this game. She'd seduced him while he was camouflaged to get him to see she knew his secret. The only reason she'd ever step so far out of her box of inhibitions was to prod him to trust her.

He hadn't told her his secret, and he'd hidden his duty to protect her. Frustration and hurt tightened like a fist around her heart.

"Why can't you tell me the truth?" Her anger had drained, along with her energy, but disappointment burned hot and bitter in her throat as she attempted to hold back more tears.

He rolled from her, levered himself up, and strode to the bathroom. He returned and sat on the edge of the bed.

His mouth drew to a hard line, and the muscle

that twitched when he was unhappy or angry jumped like crazy beneath the skin of his jaw.

She drew the sheet up to her chin, needing the cover since he'd retreated from her with his warmth. "I know it's not some top-secret, military-issue camo armor you wear to disappear." She lost the battle with the tears and they ran unchecked down her cheeks. "Tell me, Trevor. I deserve to know the truth."

Yeah, she deserved to know the truth. How much to tell her remained the problem. How much to divulge without losing her but still protecting himself and his kind.

Damn her tears. She wasn't using them to control him. She wasn't like that. She'd tried to hold them back. He understood her emotions as well as he knew her body and its responses to him. His mind no longer questioned his fate. She was his mate.

Fuck me! Why have the Fates chosen this woman, this human for me?

He needed a Watcher female, someone he could be his true self with, in all his forms. He didn't want to scare Cassie, nor did he want her pity. He was proud of his heritage, but this situation was too complicated.

His mate. His mate who sat propped up against the pillows awaiting his response. Answer her question. The simplest one.

"I'm a para. Paranormal."

She narrowed her eyes but said nothing.

"I can disappear, creating a reflective field around me, camouflaging my body."

She glanced down at the sheets, her fingers rubbing the fabric as she chewed her bottom lip. Her brow furrowed, and she cocked her mouth to one side in the way she always did when considering a problem.

She locked her gaze on his, her chin lifting and firming. "So, I wasn't crazy, and I didn't just see things. And that's what you did the first day I was here?"

He stayed very still, assessing her mood. Her fingers gripped the sheet, and her nostrils flared. She was building a head of steam, and he tried to prepare for the questions she might have.

"Why did you scare the shit out of me that day?"

He kept his voice calm, even though a dozen butterflies fought to escape his stomach. "Paras arrive through a very loud portal, not on the ferry with humans. I had to keep the secret."

"And now that I know there are others like you? What now?"

"I have to ask you to keep that secret."

She squinted at him and ground her teeth.

Oh, shit, here it comes. He knew a pissed off woman when he saw one.

"Even though you don't trust me?"

Hitting him with a sledgehammer would have hurt less. The pain in her eyes stabbed him straight to the heart. He'd caused her this pain.

"Why do you say that?"

What a stupid, stupid question!

Her lip trembled as a sob broke free. Anger, disappointment, and pure outrage boiled over in her words. "You slept with me as a convenience. To keep me close. To make your fucking job easier!" She stood, shaking, as she pulled the sheet free to wrap around her. "I heard you. I heard that woman with

Sage say that you found an easier way to keep track of me. That it was easier to know where I am when I'm beneath you in bed. I believe she said something like 'easier to know where your sheath is when your dagger's in it.'"

How could she believe that?

As he raked his hand through his hair, angry with himself, furious with his predicament, he admitted, given the evidence, he'd have to believe the same.

Chapter Seven

She'd kicked him out of her room and out of her life.

Of course, she had. He'd have done the same if he were in her shoes. He invisibly waited for a human to come along and punch the down button for the elevator.

Why did fate have to choose a human for my mate?

Why can't I just fucking tell her who and what I am?

Frustrated and having no answers, he slid into the elevator when a couple, obviously in love—or lust—happened by. He turned from them as they engaged in a hot kiss that made his belly twist and his heart ache for his Cassie.

Mine.

What was his problem? Every time he decided to stay away from her, she dragged him back in.

Not true. He wanted her more than he wanted his next breath. He needed her. Taking a deep breath, he vanished and raced to where he knew he'd find answers.

***

"Thanks for coming with me, Cassidy."

Dana sounded short of breath as they walked along the marked path through the shady woods. She rubbed her very round belly.

Cassidy's heart squeezed painfully and, for a moment, she couldn't speak. What she wouldn't do to be like that with Trevor—so totally in love and in tune with a man. If only he'd give her the chance, but she couldn't force him to trust her, and she wouldn't lay her heart on the line.

She'd agreed to go with Dana to the far boat dock to get her mind off Trevor.

"It's really no problem, Dana. I needed the diversion."

Dana paused for a moment, her hands bracing her lower back as she stretched. She cocked her head and surveyed the trees.

I don't see anything. Maybe living with paras made Dana more in tune, or maybe she is a para, too?

"Dana, are you...?" How to ask the question? *Spit it out.* "Are you a para?"

Dana's eyebrows shot up as she faced Cassie with a crooked smile.

"So, Trevor finally told you?"

"Not everything. Not enough."

"Give him some time, honey. He'll come around."

"Whatever you noticed in the trees? They're probably Trevor." Cassidy shrugged as they continued along the path, irritated he would follow her. If he was so worried about what she was doing, he should've told her the whole truth.

She shook her head, trying to dislodge her wannabe lover from her brain. She was so distracted, she totally missed seeing the creep step right in front of her. She plowed right into the sleaze who had tried, unsuccessfully, to single her out several times since she'd been here.

Strong hands manacled her arms.

Embarrassed she'd been so intent on Trevor that she'd slammed into the "professor," she sputtered an apology. Her eyes met his, cold as ice, black as sin. She gasped and, when he sneered, recognized the danger she'd missed before. A shiver streaked up her spine as he dug his fingers into her flesh, trapping her like an animal.

Her heart pounding, she glanced at Dana. While her friend's eyes were wide, she seemed calm. She twisted the ring on her left hand around and around, and her lips moved silently, as if in prayer.

Satisfied Dana wasn't stressed enough to go into premature labor, Cassidy fervently wished, for once, that Trevor were watching her.

"Let me go." She yanked her arms. He released her suddenly, leaving her to rub her soon-to-be-bruised forearms.

"My apologies, Ms. Sinclair."

He bowed slightly and moved slowly behind her along the path.

Wait, how did he know her name? *I never told him my name—*

The cold edge of the knife pressed lightly against her throat.

Dana gasped and ordered, "Let her go."

The son of a bitch barked a harsh laugh in her ear, his breath hot and moist on her neck. "I don't think so. This woman is worth a lot of money to me." He wrapped one arm around her waist, pulling her against him while she fought back useless tears. "You, my dear," he said, addressing Dana, "will bring a considerable bonus. Come on, both of you, nice and easy, to the dock."

"You need to reconsider what you're doing," Dana warned as he herded her down the path, Cassidy still in his grasp. "You won't get away with whatever you're planning."

An evil smile curved his face as he replied, "No one even knows you're out here, and nobody uses this pier, so I think I'm already home free."

***

After a few minutes of running with the breeze in his face, the boughs slapping harmlessly against his furry arms and legs, Trevor realized he fought a battle already lost.

She was his. Period. And he was definitely hers.

In fact, she was nearby in the forest with Rekkus's mate, Dana. He'd heard their voices, but, not detecting any stress in their conversation, he'd moved on. Cassie had been clear she wanted to be left alone. He'd give her time to burn off some of her anger before he approached her again. He stayed at the boundaries of hearing them.

The tone of their voices changed suddenly. He broke out in a cold sweat under his fur. He shifted back to human form and fought the fear that threatened to paralyze him. While his pulse raced, he focused on controlling his breathing. He needed to calm down to control his innate abilities to cloak and track silently.

My mate's life may depend on it. Completely alert now, sensing danger, he cloaked himself and moved in their direction.

A male had joined them. The voice sounded like the man's he'd seen with Cassie. Maybe he was harassing her. The man needed a lesson, and Trevor was just the one to teach it. He smiled. Maybe he could win some points back with Cassie with his chivalry—

That thought flew right out of his mind when he spied the huge black tiger racing toward the women's location.

If Rekkus was responding as a tiger, the women were definitely in trouble.

He made his way silently, invisibly, to cut off the man's escape. The dock was not typically used by the island staff.

Probably a boat there to get away. And some small hole in the island's defense system has been discovered.

A tiger's roar rent the air. Why hadn't he heard the man's pained cries?

He heard the bastard's smug laughter as Dana said, "Don't hurt her."

Oh, fuck. He couldn't move fast enough, but he had to keep his composure, had to calm his natural desire to protect his mate.

There. Rekkus in his black tiger form prowling lethally between Dana and the attacker. And Cassie with a knife glinting at her throat.

He froze.

Think. One deep breath and then another. He was trained to do this, but the stakes had never been so damn high. If he made one mistake, he could lose her.

He wouldn't make a mistake.

Cassie's life hung in the balance.

Breathe, Cassidy. She tried not to move a muscle, fully and uncomfortably aware of the cold steel at her throat. The sharp edge pinched her skin, microns from slicing into her neck. Her muscles cramped holding her chin up and away from the blade as she fought against her sickening fear. Sweat dripped into her eyes, burning them.

The black tiger paced before her, muscles bunched. It growled, baring its teeth, warning the eerie professor to stay away from Dana. Glittering golden eyes narrowed at the attacker, never leaving its prey.

Something about those eyes.... Ah! Dana's mate, Rekkus, is a shifter. Hope flickered but Cassidy forced her thoughts to the asshole holding her.

How am I going to get out of this? Why does he want me, of all people?

She waited for an opportunity to get free or talk him out of whatever the hell he was planning. What did he say? She was worth a lot of money? Who would pay for her to be kidnapped? Or worse, killed?

The thought chilled her. She closed her eyes for a moment to center herself and, when she opened them, she caught Dana's gaze dart for a second to a location behind her. From her friend's single raised eyebrow she knew Trevor lay in wait to strike. Could he save her?

"Come on. We have to go. Now."

He yanked her back, away from the prowling black beast. She couldn't hold back the yelp as the knife bit into her skin, but she managed to get a hand on his forearm. Trying to remain calm and loose, ready for whenever Trevor attacked, for she was sure he would, she moved carefully along with her captor. Rekkus and Dana followed, though she remained behind her tiger-shifting mate.

The tang of salt water and sea grass on the breeze grew stronger. Her time grew short. Soon, she'd have to fight for her life. Her blood mixed with her perspiration and trailed warm down her neck and between her breasts. He pressed her body to his. She had to swallow the bile that rose in her throat when his erection rubbed against her back. *The bastard is aroused.* She couldn't pull away with the blade at her neck.

The pier appeared at the end of the path. Maybe Trevor wasn't there. Maybe this madman would take her to God only knew where and kill her or, worse, turn her over to human traffickers. She'd rather die than become a slave to some bastard's sexual depravities.

She couldn't take that chance.

As her captor tried to transition her to the boat, distracted by the tiger on the dock ready to pounce, Cassidy pushed with all her might against the hand holding the knife. She latched onto the knife, feeling the sharp sting as the blade sliced deeply into her palm.

A roar exploded from behind her. A hairy creature like the one she'd seen for the briefest of moments during the school shooting leaped from the boat.

He crashed onto the stunned man.

Her attacker let her go, and she fell back into the boat, blood spurting from her hand.

The scene blurred as relief and pain flooded through her. Calmer voices now filled her ears as the afternoon sunlight filtered through the overhanging leaves.

"Cassie," she barely heard as her vision narrowed and grayed. "I've got you, baby. I've got you."

Lifted by familiar, strong male arms, she let go, knowing she was secure and safe as everything went black.

Chapter Eight

"What did you find out?" Trevor asked Cemil, Rekkus, and Cyrus as they filed into the lobby where he paced like a caged animal. Sage and Dana had been with Cassie in the staff lounge for over an hour now, and he anxiously and impatiently waited for one of them to tell him her condition.

"Well, his name is Phillip Jeffries, and he is human," Cyrus said.

"I still can't get over how I didn't sense his intention. It just shows how dedicated that group is to infiltrate the island." Cemil hung his head, obviously taking the blame.

Cyrus patted his brother's back. "This was well planned, Cemil. It is not your fault. We will have to tighten up security and let the Syndicate know of the latest threat. Mr. Branson needs to know of the specific threat to his son."

Something about the frown between Cyrus's brows bothered Trevor. "What do you mean, specific threat?"

"The attack on the school was not to assassinate Allan Branson, but rather to abduct him." He paused before adding, "And his teacher."

Shock and fury seared his vision for a brief moment. "You mean they planned to *kidnap* Allan and Cassie?"

"Yes," Rekkus said. "And there's more."

Cyrus' nostrils flared while his jaw clenched. "This new group, the Mundus Novus, planned to use the boy to obtain information to further their ambitions. He's a clairvoyant empath. Very valuable to vermin like them."

Stealing the boy from his father made Trevor's stomach turn. The boy was motherless already and had bonded with Cassie as his surrogate mother. His empathy had become a curse, and he'd retreated to an emotionless world. She was the only one he'd let penetrate the shell he'd lived in since his mother had died.

"So, based on their surveillance, they determined they needed Cassie to communicate with him, to get him to do their bidding," Trevor said.

Bastards. He needed to see her now more than ever to reassure himself she was okay. Otherwise, he'd kill that son of a bitch. No matter how well protected the prisoner, he'd make that asshole pay if Cassie's injury left her permanently disabled.

"What did he want with Dana?"

Rekkus stalked away.

"He planned to turn her over to the Mundus Novus, who he thought would kill her once she gave birth. If this is the faction that put the bounty on Cyrus, they would surely kill her as payback to Rekkus," Cemil said, his fist clenching in restrained fury. "Rekkus saved Cyrus when he was targeted for helping the Syndicate take down immoral sects. Jeffries figured they would raise the baby in their ideology."

Trevor gritted teeth. "And he is still living?"

"He is," Cemil said, clearly angry, though the least demonstrative of the three. "He is secured and awaiting transport via the portal to the Syndicate, who will continue debriefing him."

I'd like to debrief him. Calm down. Focus on getting to Cassie. Destroy the Mundus Novus later.

"Can you take me to Cassie?" he asked Cemil. "I need to see her."

The man's anger dropped, and a crooked grin tugged at the corner of his mouth. "You need to see your intended mate, Trevor? Why have you not told her everything? Why haven't you mated with her? Look at Rekkus, how complete he is."

"I really don't feel like getting into this right now. Can you take me to her or not?"

Cemil exchanged a wry look with Cyrus and Rekkus before shrugging. "Sure. Follow me."

***

With her right hand covered with a poultice that smelled like a football player's week-old gym socks, Cassidy had a problem opening the letter Sage handed her. Frustrated, she dropped the envelope on the blanket that covered her and flopped back against the pillows of the couch in the staff lounge.

"Just read it, will you?" she huffed to Sage.

Sage retrieved the envelope but seemed uncomfortable opening the message.

"Go ahead, I'm sure it's not personal."

Sage exchanged a glance with Dana, who shrugged a shoulder. Sarka remained near the window, stirring her tea absently.

Sage read:

My dearest Cassidy,

I hope you are well. I expect by now you will have learned of the existence of our kind, paranormal races. You have been such an integral part of Allan's recovery and, more importantly his life. He loves you, and I believe you love him.

After spending time with you this last week, I would like to make you a proposition. Please come live with Allan and me. It would make him so happy; you alone have been able to reach him since he witnessed his mother's murder.

It would make me happy, too. I believe we are compatible and could become good friends. If this concept makes you uncomfortable, please do not turn down my offer. My son is the most important thing in my life. I'd like you to consider that we'd make Allan loving parents.

Ian Branson

Sarka, who'd barely spoken two words since Cassidy regained consciousness, sputtered out her tea. "He's proposing marriage? Through a fecking letter? Asshat."

Oddly, the idea did not repulse Cassidy. She did love Allan, and she liked his father. And the one man she truly loved didn't trust her. She didn't have anything to lose.

As if conjuring him with a single thought, Trevor appeared just inside the archway.

Her pulse raced, and her chest tightened. She

forced air into lungs that didn't want to work properly. Tension hung heavy into the room as she waited for him to say something.

"Cassidy."

Oh, no. He hadn't called her that all week. So formal, like—

Like he'd heard Sage read the letter.

Cassidy stared at his face, his brow pinched, his Adam's apple jumping.

Oh, yeah. He'd heard. Her heart ached that she'd hurt him. She hated hurting anyone, but he'd made his choice not to trust her.

Her inner voice scolded her. She wasn't being fair. He'd only known her a few days; he was only protecting his family. And she hadn't been honest with him, either. He didn't know she'd seen him in his Watcher form the day of the school attack. How could a man pass a test he didn't know he was taking?

Still, Mr. Branson—Ian—offered her a comfortable, stable life.

A life without love.

Would that be enough?

***

So Branson offered her a new life with him, essentially offering her a marriage of convenience. Using his son like a fucking carrot.

Well, she was his.

"Would you all give me a few minutes with Cassidy?"

Not breaking eye contact with Cassie, Trevor waited as everyone moved out of the lounge. She was pale, having lost a significant amount of blood. His stomach twisted painfully that he'd missed the signals and put her in danger again.

Cassie—his sweet Cassie—bit her bottom lip and picked at the edge of the bandage until it frayed. She knew he'd heard the contents of the letter. She no longer met his gaze, rubbing the edges of the blanket nervously with the wrist of her unbandaged hand.

"I want to thank you—" she began before he cut her off.

"Don't thank me, Cassie." He paced toward the door then turned back to face her. "Don't thank me. If I'd done what I should have, you wouldn't be hurt."

Her soft voice broke his heart. "You don't know that. He was willing to do whatever it took to get me. Apparently, I'm worth a lot of money to someone."

"Cassie...."

"Trevor, you don't have to say anything. I don't blame you."

"Are you considering Branson's offer?" His heart thudded loudly in his ears as he waited for her response.

"It's not your concern."

"The hell it isn't!" She wasn't going to dismiss him from her life. He wouldn't let her. He couldn't let her.

Her eyes widened with surprise.

"I want you to listen to me for five minutes. Just let me have my say. Then you can tell me to go to hell if you want."

The five seconds he waited for her to nod were the longest of his life.

"Okay. I've been an idiot. I know that." He paced away, avoiding her gaze, afraid of seeing her anger, or worse, indifference. "You know I'm a paranormal.

You know I'm able to disappear from human view. But my biggest secret is that I'm a Watcher."

She confused him when her only response was to raise an eyebrow.

"Is that another word for Bigfoot or Sasquatch?"

He firmed his jaw, pride straightening his spine. "Yes. We prefer Watcher. We are very secretive for obvious reasons."

"Because you are hunted by humans."

Again, a statement, not a question. More curiosity and acceptance than surprise or disgust.

"Yes."

"At least you finally told me."

"What do you mean, 'finally?'"

A sad smile crooked the corner of her mouth. "I've known since the day of the attack at the school."

"I don't remember shifting that day."

"It was only a split second, but I saw you shift when you were shot."

"You came to me, while I was bleeding out on the floor, knowing what I am?" Shock flashed through him like the time he'd grabbed an electric fence.

"I didn't care."

"Didn't?" Past tense. Damn it. Had he fucked up too many times for her to forgive?

Cassie's eyes filled, and her lower lip wobbled, but she didn't answer. Anger he could take, and preferred, but her silence and tears stabbed at his heart.

"Oh, baby, you've known all along and didn't say anything?"

"I was waiting for you to trust me enough to tell me yourself. But you never did," she whispered, her words spilling out. She turned her head away, sobs racking her body.

An idiot. He was an absolute idiot not to see his future right in front of him from the beginning. Somehow, he had to make her see. On his knees, he gently tipped her chin so she had to look at him.

"I'm so sorry, baby. I should have told you. I was afraid you'd see a freak, not a man with another side to my soul."

Her eyes glistened with unshed tears and her lower lip trembled. Was she still considering Branson's proposal? Or opening her heart to him?

Come on, Greene, time to lay it on the line.

"I love you and want you in my life. I need you in my life, and I can't imagine living without you. Please give me a chance."

Gently, he pulled her into his arms, holding her as she cried, every tear a spike in his heart. On the floor, with Cassie in his lap, he enfolded her, waiting out the storm.

Finally, she eased back, sniffled, and punched him in the shoulder.

He shouldn't have, but he couldn't help the smile that broke free. A frown creased her brow as her eyes narrowed. "You think this is funny?"

A chuckle burst forth, followed by outright laughter. He shouldn't be laughing, but he was relieved she felt some passion for him, even if it was anger.

Cassie hit him again and again, and all he could do was laugh and let her expend all her anger on him.

Suddenly, she was laughing, too, though she kept punching him.

Relief and passion flooded him. No longer was he laughing. Pulling her close, he brushed her mouth with his.

She sighed. *Oh, by the gods, let me not mess this up!*

When her lips parted, inviting his invasion, he growled and his tongue swept in. He found her just as hungry as he was and let her take the lead. His hands tangled in her hair while her lips traveled along his jaw and his neck then nipped at his earlobe.

He wanted her. Now.

But not here in this public room.

Gently, he pulled back and cradled her face in his hands. Searching her passion-glazed eyes, he waited until they cleared and focused on him.

"Cassie. I need you, baby."

A seductive smile curved her kiss-swollen lips, and she tried to pull him back into her embrace. "I need you, too."

He held her at arm's length. "No, I mean I need you in my life forever."

She frowned.

What is she thinking? Maybe she doesn't want to be mated with a freak....

"Be specific."

He frowned and cocked his head at her. "I want you to be my mate."

Several moments went by.

"Is that what paras call a spouse?"

She sure knew how to tie him in knots. Could he survive a lifetime of such treatment?

Hell, yeah!

"Yes. We mate for life. If you prefer, I can call you my wife."

Her brilliant smile eased the tension in his throat, and he released the breath he hadn't been aware he'd been holding. Leaning in, she kissed him gently before snuggling against his chest. *She belongs right here, in my arms.*

Her voice was muffled against his shirt, but what he heard caused his soul to sing.

"You can call me your wife with my family and your mate with your family."

He pressed a kiss to her hair. "Will you do it now?"

She jerked slightly but didn't move away from the haven of his embrace. "Here?"

She sounded scandalized, but not unwilling. His blood surged in his veins at her misconception. "No, baby, not mating in the sexual sense. Though I'd like to make that happen as soon as we get to someplace private."

He moved back so he could look into her eyes. *I love her so much. Let this be easy for her*, he prayed. The ritual involved releasing one's soul to mate with another's, physically close to death. He'd heard of humans who had almost died because they'd panicked.

"When we mate, it's our souls joining. You have to trust me." He caressed her cheek. "Will you?"

She nodded, fresh tears shimmering in her eyes.

"Are you afraid?"

Her watery smile dispelled his fear. "No. I just never thought you'd want me, need me." She touched his stubbly cheek with the fingertips of her uninjured hand. "What do I have to do?"

He couldn't help but smile. Always brave in the face of the unknown.

"I'll kiss you, and you will lose yourself in the kiss."

"I can do that."

"Then, allow your soul to float free. My soul will find yours and unite." Serious, he gazed deeply into her eyes. "You may feel lightheaded or even that you can't breathe, I'm told. But I'm here. You're safe with me."

She nodded as he took one hand in his and grasped the forearm of her bandaged hand. "I know."

Slowly, he lowered his head, his lips grazing hers at first. Then he deepened the kiss. She took a deep breath. In his mind's eye, he walked into a fogbank. He searched for her. He found her in a shimmering golden light. He embraced her, their souls touching, uniting.

She relaxed against him. Their mating had been gentle. Exactly the way he'd wanted.

Breaking the kiss, he leaned back to gaze down at his mate. A soft smile curved her lips, and her lashes fluttered open to reveal eyes full of love.

"So, when do I get to meet your family?"

No one made him laugh like she did. "Is tomorrow soon enough? The ferry will take us back to the mainland then we'll head home."

She snuggled against him as he lifted her and headed for the lobby. "Where are you taking me?"

He kissed her gently as he strode past the group of cheering staff members, grinning at their congratulations. "To get started making our own family."

About the Author

Carolyn Spear was raised in a rural Tidewater Virginia, the kind of place where everyone knows everyone. While she's moved around the Eastern Seaboard, she's back home in Tidewater, married with two teenage girls and a pampered princess of a dog.

As a teenager, she sneaked her mother's Barbara Cartland romances. These historical romances full of dashing British rogues and spirited ingenues opened a door to another world. Now, years later, Carolyn's mission is to introduce readers to her world.

For more about Carolyn and her works-in-progress, visit http://www.carolynspearromance.com/

Book List

Sorcerer's Legacy (Wiccan Haus #12)

Book List

www.ingramcontent.com/pod-product-compliance
Lightning Source LLC
Chambersburg PA
CBHW060944120626
46557CB00003B/1134